PERCY JACKSON & THE OLYMPIANS
BOOK ONE

THE LIGHTNING THIEF

The Graphic Novel

by
RICK RIORDAN

Adapted by
Robert Venditti

Art by
Attila Futaki

Color by
José Villarrubia

Layouts by
Orpheus Collar

Lettering by
Chris Dickey

DISNEP · HYPERION
Los Angeles   New York

YOU NEVER SHOULD HAVE BEEN BORN.

"YOU SEE, THE WAR HAD BEEN THE RESULT OF A *SPAT* BETWEEN THE SONS OF ZEUS AND POSEIDON ON ONE SIDE, AND THE SONS OF HADES ON THE OTHER.

YOU *REALLY* NEED TO WORK ON YOUR DELIVERY.

AFTER WORLD WAR II, THE THREE SONS OF KRONOS--ZEUS, POSEIDON, AND HADES--MADE A PACT NEVER TO SIRE ANY MORE HALF-BLOODS.

THEIR OFFSPRING WERE AFFECTING THE COURSE OF HUMAN EVENTS TOO MUCH.

"SO THE BROTHERS SWORE AN OATH ON THE *RIVER STYX*, AND THE PACT WAS UPHELD...

"...UNTIL SEVENTEEN YEARS AGO. ZEUS FELL OFF THE WAGON, AS IT WERE, AND HAD A *DAUGHTER* WITH AN AMERICAN TV STARLET.

"THE CHILD'S NAME WAS THALIA, AND SHE WAS TWELVE WHEN HADES LEARNED OF HER. FURIOUS, HE LOOSED HIS WORST MONSTERS TO DESTROY HER.

"A *SATYR* WAS DISPATCHED TO BRING HER SAFELY TO CAMP. THEY--AND TWO OTHER HALF-BLOODS THEY MET ALONG THE WAY--*NEARLY* MADE IT.

"WOUNDED AND WEARY OF THE CHASE, THALIA MADE HER FINAL STAND JUST OUTSIDE THE VALLEY, SACRIFICING HERSELF SO THAT HER COMPANIONS COULD MAKE IT TO SAFETY."

AS SHE PERISHED, ZEUS TOOK PITY ON HER AND TRANSFORMED HER INTO A PINE TREE. HER SPIRIT PROTECTS THE CAMP'S BORDERS TO THIS DAY.

JUST EAST OF ST. LOUIS.
JUNE 13.

8 DAYS UNTIL THE SUMMER
SOLSTICE AND AN OLYMPIAN
BATTLE ROYAL ENSUES.

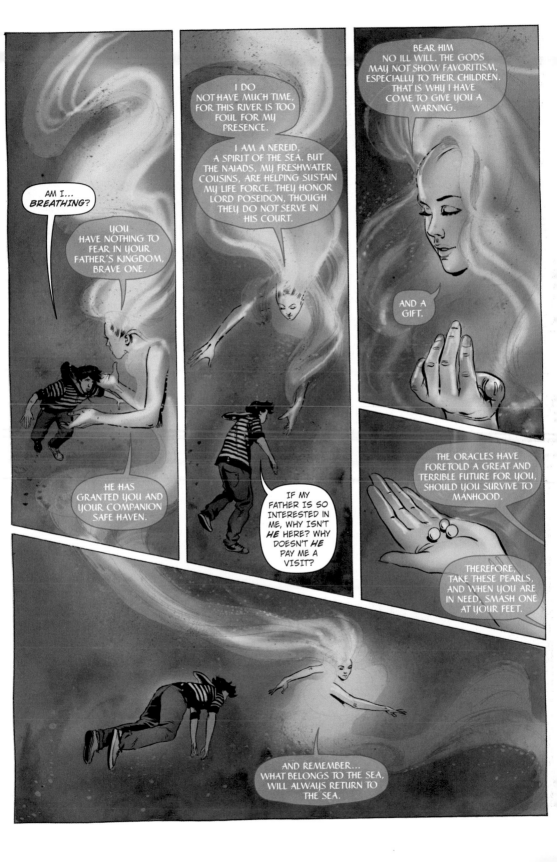

DO YOU ACCEPT THE CHARGES?

UM...YES?

PLEASE HOLD.

PERCY!

SORRY ABOUT CALLING COLLECT, BUT I DIDN'T KNOW WHERE YOU WERE. JUST DON'T FORGET TO PAY THE BILL -- IRIS HAS BEEN KNOWN TO CUT PEOPLE'S SERVICE.

LUKE? WHAT *IS* THIS? WHO'S IRIS?

THE GODDESS OF RAINBOWS. SHE CARRIES MESSAGES FOR US SOMETIMES. CELL PHONES ARE TOO EASY FOR MONSTERS TO TRACK.

SO WHAT'S YOUR PROGRESS? WORD LEAKED OUT BACK HERE ABOUT THE ZEUS-POSEIDON STANDOFF, AND IT'S SHAPING UP TO BE THE TROJAN WAR ALL OVER AGAIN. THE CAMPERS ARE AT EACH OTHERS' THROATS.

WE'RE IN DENVER. NOT TOO BAD, CONSIDERING. CHIMERAS AND FURIES AND ANNABETH, OH MY...

-:SCARF:-

-:CHOMP:-

-:MMPF:-

YOU BIG SPENDERS READY FOR YOUR CHECK?

SET 'EM UP AGAIN, DOLL.

MY TREAT.

R-RIGHT AWAY, SIR.

SO YOU'RE THE *WATERBOY*, HUH? HEARD YOU BUSTED CLARISSE'S SPEAR.

SO WHAT? YOU COME HERE LOOKING TO GET SOMETHING OF *YOURS* BUSTED?

MAY WE... UM...TALK TO YOUR BOSS?

PLEASE?

THAT'S AS CLOSE AS WE'RE GOING TO GET TO AN INVITATION.

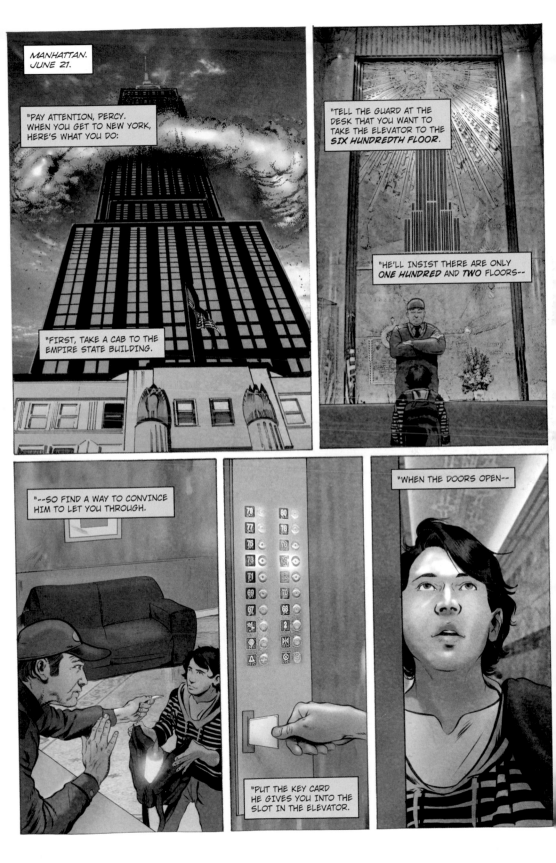

"--YOU'LL BE AT THE **HOME OF THE GODS.**

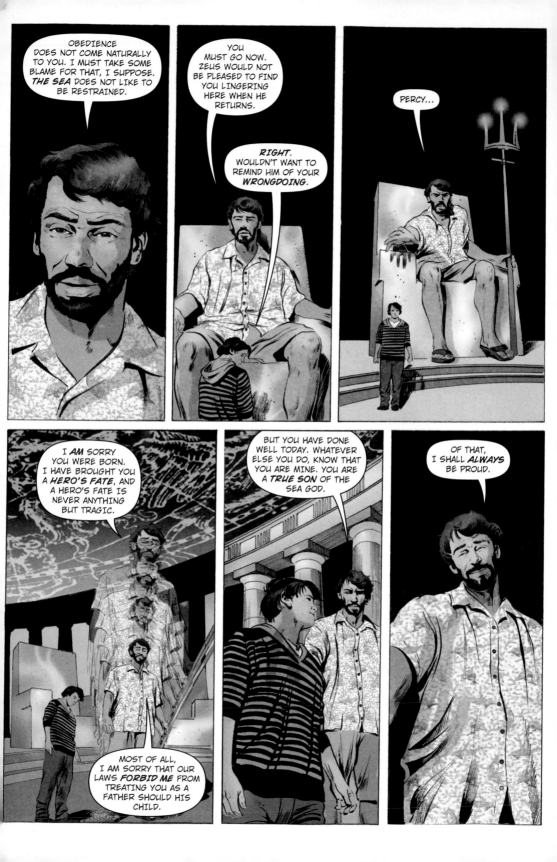

Adapted from the novel
Percy Jackson & the Olympians, Book One: The Lightning Thief

Text copyright © 2010 by Rick Riordan
Illustrations copyright © 2010 Disney Enterprises, Inc.

Design by Jim Titus
Edited by Christian Trimmer

Printed in the United States of America
FAC-038091-19025
First Edition, October 2010
16 15 14
ISBN 978-1-4231-1696-7 (hardcover)

ISBN 978-1-4231-1710-0 (paperback)
Library of Congress Control Number For The Hardcover And Paperback Editions: 2010035512.

Visit www.readriordan.com
and www.DisneyBooks.com